T0193280

NUTMEG'S STORY

Believe in Yourself

To order additional copies of this book, contact:
Xlibris
844-714-8691
www.Xlibris.com
Orders@Xlibris.com

ISBN: Softcover   978-1-6698-2363-6
         EBook   978-1-6698-2362-9

Print information available on the last page

Rev. date: 09/20/2022

NUTMEG'S STORY

Believe in Yourself

Andie Campbell

DEDICATION:

To Megahn Howard, for her help brainstorming
these characters all those years ago.

ha
ha
ha

vi

Once upon a time, there was a little squirrel named Nutmeg. She was lively and clever as most squirrels tend to be, but there was one thing that was special about this little squirrel. This little squirrel believed she could fly, and she told her friends so.

"I can fly," she said.

However, her friend Hercules the tiger was not buying it. "You can't fly any more than Bananas can fly," he said, and he threw a banana at Bananas the gorilla.

"Hey!" Bananas growled, throwing the peel back at Hercules, while Monica the mockingbird was laughing hysterically at the whole thing--that is until Hercules threw a banana at her, that is.

"I can fly!" Nutmeg insisted, turning to the last of her friends, Sunflower, a small white rabbit, her eyes pleading. "You believe me, don't you, Sunflower?"

Sunflower's eyes darted from Nutmeg to her other friends and then back to Nutmeg before she finally shook her head. "Squirrels can't fly."

Nutmeg looked hopefully at each of her friends in turn, but they were not paying any attention to her anymore. Bananas and Hercules were throwing bananas back and forth at each other, and the two girls were watching them. "The phoenix believes I can fly!" Nutmeg finally burst out, desperate for someone, anyone, to believe her.

They all looked over at her. "Phoenixes aren't real," said Hercules, who threw another banana at Bananas. They all turned back to the banana tossing, but Nutmeg was not about to be deterred that easily.

"The phoenix is real, and I can take you to her."

6

This caught Hercules' interest. "Oh, really?" He glanced at the others before turning back to her. "Sure, why not? So where does this phoenix live?" He asked once they were on their way.

"Up high in the mountains." Nutmeg's tone was solemn and serious.

"Up high in the mountains," echoed Monica giggling, but Nutmeg either did not notice or chose to ignore her.

Up and up and up they climbed far into the mountains. The animals were beginning to get nervous. Just where was Nutmeg leading them?

"I want to go home." Sunflower was trembling and terrified and hid behind Bananas as they climbed.

"We're almost there." It was not that Nutmeg was not aware of her friends' discomfort, but the thought of being able to finally prove her ability to fly was just too exciting for her.

Soon they came to a clearing.

"Who dares enter my lair?" Came a deep voice.

Nutmeg bounded forward. "Hi, Phoenix, it's me, Nutmeg."

A shadow shown from behind a rock, shrinking as this mysterious phoenix stepped forward out of the shadows. Although the phoenix was much larger than Nutmeg, Sunflower, and Monica, she had nothing on either Bananas or Hercules in size. In fact, she hardly looked like any threat at all. She was old and scraggly, appearing half-blind, her feathers falling out even as she hobbled forward. "Nutmeg. Back so soon?"

"Nutmeg?" Sunflower's eyes were big and wide.

"Phoenix, I was just telling my friends what you said--that I can fly."

"Is it true?" Sunflower peered up at her from behind Bananas.

"Of course it's true," the Phoenix replied.

"I don't believe you," Hercules insisted. "I don't even think you're really a Phoenix either. You're just some old bird!"

He stood there waiting for her to reply, but she said nothing, instead, she burst into flames and in mere seconds was reduced to ash.

"Told you," he said with a shrug and turned to go.

"No, wait!" Nutmeg cried after him. "She's a phoenix! They burst into flame and then are reborn from their ashes!"

"Yeah, right."

"Hercules, look!" Monica said quietly, awe in her voice.

Hercules and the others turned to look, and sure enough, there was a baby bird peering out from the ashes.

The animals stared until Sunflower finally broke the silence. "I wanna see Nutmeg fly."

"What?" Hercules shook his head in disbelief. "You can't possibly believe this." But the other animals were nodding along with Sunflower.

Nutmeg just stared at them wide-eyed.

"You can do it," the baby phoenix urged, its voice suddenly high pitched rather than deep and gravelly.

Nutmeg nodded and turned to her friends who lifted her onto their shoulders and tossed her into the air. Gracefully, Nutmeg glided over the trees until she slowly floated back down towards her friends. Nutmeg was the very first flying squirrel.

Printed in the United States
by Baker & Taylor Publisher Services